THE TOWER IN
HO-HO WOOD
AND OTHER STORIES

The Tower in Ho-Ho Wood

and Other Stories

by
ENID BLYTON

Illustrated by
Lesley Blackman

AWARD PUBLICATIONS

For further information on Enid Blyton please conatct
www.blyton.com

ISBN 1–84135–463-5

First Published by Award Publications Limited 1989
This edition first published 2006

Published by Award Publications Limited, The Old Riding
School, Welbeck Estate, Worksop, Notts. S80 3LR

Printed in Singapore

CONTENTS

The Enchanted Gloves

Ho-Ho and Higgledy were two little brownies who lived in Sunflower Cottage on the edge of Honey Common. One was a painter and the other was a carpenter. Ho-Ho could paint a wall or a door in double-quick time, and Higgledy could make anything you pleased, from a giant's table to a canary's bath.

One day they had a message from Long-Beard, the Chancellor of Fairyland. He lived in a palace nearby, and the two brownies often saw him out in his golden carriage.

Ho-Ho opened the letter, and read it out loud to Higgledy. This is what it said:

'The chancellor would be glad if

Ho-Ho and Higgledy would call at his palace tomorrow morning to do some work.'

'Ha!' said Higgledy, pleased. 'That's fine! We shall get well paid for that! And it will be lovely to say that we work for the chancellor. All our friends will know then that we are good workmen.'

The next morning the brownies went to the palace. Long-Beard the chancellor saw them, and told them that he wanted his dining-room painted yellow, and a new bookshelf made for his study.

'Very good, sir,' said Ho-Ho and Higgledy. 'We will start straight away.'

They began their work, whistling merrily. Cinders, the chancellor's black cat, and Snowie, his white dog, came to watch them. They sat solemnly there and watched everything that the brownies did.

'Do go away,' said Ho-Ho at last. 'You make us feel quite uncomfortable, staring all day like that.'

'We like to watch you,' said Cinders.

'What a lovely colour that yellow is that you are using, Ho-Ho.'

'I wish my tail was that colour,' said Snowie the dog. 'I hate being all white, and Snowie is such a silly name.'

'Well, it's just as bad being all black,' said Cinders. 'It's very dull. Now if I were striped yellow, I should feel grand.'

'Will you have any paint left over when you have finished your job, Ho-Ho?' asked the dog.

'I might,' said Ho-Ho. 'But if you think I'm going to waste it on you, you're very much mistaken.'

'Yes, but the chancellor would be so pleased,' said Cinders. 'I'm sure he's tired of seeing us all one colour. He might pay you double for being so kind.'

'I don't know about that,' said Higgledy. 'I've heard the chancellor isn't very generous.'

'Snowie! Cinders! Come and have your dinners!' called a voice. The two animals ran off and Ho-Ho and Higgledy went on with their work.

The next day and the next Snowie and Cinders came and watched the two brownies, and on the third day, when Ho-Ho had finished painting the walls a beautiful bright yellow, and Higgledy had made a very nice bookcase, the two animals went over to the paint jar. They looked into it and then spoke to Ho-Ho.

'Ho-Ho, *do* let us have the little bit of paint that's left,' begged Cinders. 'We would be glad of it and we are sure the chancellor would be pleased. Couldn't you just paint us yellow with your big brush? Do! Do!'

'Please!' said Snowie, wagging his tail hard. 'How would you like to be dressed in nothing but white all your life?'

'I shouldn't like it at all,' said Ho-Ho. 'But I don't know whether I dare to do what you want.'

The animals begged so hard that at last Ho-Ho and Higgledy gave in. Higgledy painted Snowie's long tail a most beautiful yellow, and gave him yellow ears too, and Ho-Ho painted long yellow stripes all down Cinders' black body.

They did look funny. Ho-Ho and Higgledy began to laugh when they saw how strange the two animals looked. But Cinders and Snowie were pleased. They ran out of the room and down the passage, and just round the corner they met the chancellor.

He stared in astonishment and horror at his cat and dog. Whatever could have happened to them? Was this really Snowie, with yellow ears and tail? What a horrible-looking animal! And could this really be his beautiful black cat Cinders, with long yellow stripes all down his body?

'My eyes must be going wrong!'

groaned the chancellor. 'Where are my glasses?'

He put them on and looked at the animals again – but they were still the same. What a terrible thing!

'Who has done this dreadful deed!' roared the chancellor, suddenly feeling very angry. 'Ho-Ho and Higgledy, is it you?'

He strode into the dining-room and found the two brownies there, looking rather scared.

'How dare you paint my cat and dog!' shouted Long-Beard. 'Get out of my palace at once!'

'But please, sir, Snowie and Cinders begged and begged us to,' said Ho-Ho, trembling. 'We didn't want to do it, but they said you would be pleased.'

'I don't believe you!' said the chancellor, angrily. 'You did it for a horrid joke. Go away at once and never come back!'

'We've finished our work,' said Ho-Ho, 'so we will go if you will kindly pay us, sir.'

'Pay you!' cried the chancellor. 'Not a penny piece! Not a penny piece! Ho there, servants! Come and throw these wicked brownies out.'

Two servants at once ran up, caught hold of the brownies, and threw them down the front steps of the palace. Ho-Ho and Higgledy picked themselves up and ran off in fright, leaving behind all their tools and brushes.

They didn't stop running till they came to Sunflower Cottage. Then they sat down in their little chairs and wept bitterly.

'Nasty, horrid old chancellor!' said Ho-Ho. 'We did our work. Why couldn't he have paid us? He just wanted to save the money, the mean old thing!'

'We'll pay him back somehow!' said Higgledy, drying his eyes. 'We'll go to Thumbs, the glovemaker. He's very clever, and perhaps he will think of some way to punish the mean chancellor.'

So next day they went to visit their friend, Thumbs. He made gloves – red ones, white ones, brown ones, blue ones, little and big, thin and thick. He was very clever indeed.

'Welcome!' he said, when he saw his two friends. He put down his work and set out three cups and three plates. 'We will have some biscuits and cocoa. You look sad. Tell me your trouble.'

So over their steaming cups of cocoa, Ho-Ho and Higgledy told Thumbs all about the mean chancellor, and how he had thrown them out of the palace without paying them a penny just because they had been kind enough to do what Snowie and Cinders had begged them to.

'We mean to punish the chancellor, but we can't think how to,' said Higgledy. 'You are clever, Thumbs. Can you help us?'

Thumbs put his finger on his nose and rubbed it, thinking hard. Then he began to smile.

'I've got an idea!' he said. 'It's old Long-Beard's birthday next week. I'll make him a pair of gloves and you can send them to him without saying where they come from. Inside the gloves I'll put a naughty spell. This spell will act as soon as he puts the gloves on.'

'What will it do?' asked Ho-Ho in excitement.

'Why, it will make him pinch, punch

and pull anybody who happens to be with him at the time!' said Thumbs.

'Both his hands will act so strangely he won't know what is happening! They will pull people's noses, box their ears, tickle their ribs and pinch them! Goodness, how funny it would be to watch!'

Then Ho-Ho, Higgledy and Thumbs began to laugh till the tears ran down their noses and dropped into their cocoa. Oh, what a joke it would be!

All that week Thumbs worked at the gloves. They were beautiful. Each was deep red and had little yellow buttons. They were edged with white fur and were quite the loveliest gloves that the brownies had ever seen.

When the right day came Ho-Ho and Higgledy posted the parcel to Long-Beard. They decided to take a walk near the palace on the afternoon of the chancellor's birthday, to see if they could hear what had happened.

Long-Beard had scores of parcels on his birthday. He opened them one after another, and most of them he didn't like a bit, for he was a mean old man. But when he came to the gloves – oh my! What a surprise! What magnificent gloves! How warm! Who could have sent them? There was no card in the parcel and Long-Beard puzzled hard to think who could have given him such a nice present.

It must be the king himself! he thought at last. He thinks a lot of me, and I expect he has sent me these gloves to show me how much he likes me. Well, I must wear them this afternoon, that's certain, for the king is calling for me in his carriage, and he will like to see his present on my hands.

So that afternoon, at exactly three o'clock, when the king's carriage rolled up, the chancellor stood ready to join the king. He carried his new gloves in his hand, and he meant to put them on as soon as he was in the carriage, and then the king would see them and perhaps say that he had sent them.

The carriage came, and the king leaned out to greet his chancellor.

'Come into the carriage, Long-Beard,' he said. 'It's a beautiful afternoon for a drive.'

Long-Beard stepped in and the door was closed. Just then up came Ho-Ho, Higgledy and Thumbs, out for a walk near the palace. When they saw the chancellor getting into the king's carriage with the enchanted gloves, they stood still in fright. Whatever would happen to the king when Long-Beard put on his gloves?

'Come on, we must go with the carriage!' cried Ho-Ho, and he ran after it. All three brownies swung themselves up on the ledge behind the carriage and sat there, unseen by anyone.

The chancellor put on his gloves and the king looked at them.

'What beautiful gloves,' he said – and then he gave a shout of surprise!

Long-Beard's hands had suddenly flown to the king's nose and pulled it hard! Then they went to the king's ribs and began to tickle him!

'Ooh!' cried the king. 'Ooh! Stop it! Whatever is the matter with you, Long-Beard? Have you gone mad?'

The chancellor was filled with horror. What was he doing? Why did his hands do such dreadful things? Why, they were boxing the king's ears now! He tried to put them into his pockets, but he couldn't. They flew to the king's head, knocked his crown off and pulled his hair! Then they slapped his face and pinched his cheeks!

The king grew angry, and slapped the chancellor back. Then he gave him a punch that made him gasp. The three brownies saw all that happened, for they were peeping in at the windows and they were horrified.

'Gloves, come to me!' cried Thumbs, suddenly.

At once the red gloves flew off Long-Beard's hands and went to Thumbs.

The chancellor's hands stopped behaving so queerly, and he stared at the king in shame.

The king stopped the carriage and got out.

'I must get to the bottom of this,' he said. 'What explanation have you, Long-Beard?'

'None, Your Majesty,' said Long-Beard, trembling. 'I don't know how it happened at all.'

'Well, perhaps *you* can tell me the meaning of this!' said the king, turning suddenly to the three brownies, who stood near by, red and ashamed.

'Please, Your Majesty, I will confess everything,' said Ho-Ho, and he told the king all that had happened – all about the work done at Long-Beard's palace, the cat and the dog painted yellow, and the chancellor's anger and meanness. Then he told how Thumbs had made the gloves to punish Long-Beard and the king looked stern.

'You had no right to think you could punish the chancellor yourselves,' he said. 'You should have come to me and made your complaint. You have done wrong, and you must be punished. I shall spank you myself. As for the chancellor, he did wrong too, but he has been punished enough. He must certainly pay you what he owes you, but you must give half of it to the brownies' hospital. Come here and be spanked.'

The three brownies were spanked, and then the king forgave them. The chancellor opened his purse and with very bad grace gave Ho-Ho and Higgledy what he owed them.

'You might give me ten pounds to put in the hospital box, too,' said the king to the angry chancellor. 'I'm sure it wouldn't hurt you.'

Then the carriage rolled off again and the three brownies walked home, not knowing whether to be glad or sorry.

'We'd better not be naughty any more,' said Ho-Ho at last. 'What do you think, Higgledy and Thumbs?'

'We think the same,' said his friends. So for quite half a year they were as good as gold – and after that – ah, but that's another story!

The Elm-Tree and the Willow

Side by side in the hedge grew a great elm and a sapling willow. The willow was growing in the shade of the elm, and it did not get enough light or sunshine, but it did the best it could. It sent its thin roots down into the earth to look for water, and it put out long shoots to try to reach the sunshine.

The big elm scorned the small willow. It raised its head very high in the air, it grew thousands of small leaves, and in the wind it made such a rushing noise that it drowned the voice of the little willow.

The willow sometimes spoke timidly to the tall elm. It asked the great tree questions about the birds that nested every year in the bushy trunk of the elm. It admired the pretty red blossoms that grew on the big tree's twigs in the early spring, and which it flung down to the ground when the wind blew.

'Ah, you should grow blossoms like mine!' said the elm. 'Look at your silly little green catkins! And, see – when the autumn comes I send thousands of winged fruits spinning through the air for the children to catch. They love me – I am tall and grand, my leaves shout in the wind, I give welcome shade in the hot summer – but you are a miserable little thing!'

'Well, I cannot grow very big because you take so much light and sunshine from me,' said the willow humbly. 'But, great elm-tree, I believe my roots go farther down than yours do.'

'Pooh! What do roots matter!' said the elm-tree impatiently. 'They don't show, do they?'

Now that autumn there came a great gale one dark, stormy night. The wind rushed through the trees, and the elm shouted so loudly that the willow was nearly deafened. The great tree swayed to and fro, and the willow bent, too. The wind grew wilder and wilder, and the elm shouted more and more loudly – and then suddenly a terrifying thing happened.

The great elm bent so far over that it could not get its trunk back straight again. Its poor, weak roots could not hold it, and they broke. The tree gave a loud moaning cry and toppled heavily to the ground.

The willow was left alone to bear the strong gusts of wind. It was frightened. If the elm had fallen, surely it, too, would fall, for it was but a small tree. The wind pulled hard at it, but the willow's roots were deep and held it well. When the storm at last died down, the willow was still standing – and by it lay the great elm, its leaves dying by the thousand.

The wind came by once more and whispered to the willow, 'Roots don't show, but they matter most of all! Roots don't show, but they matter most of all!'

Bad Luck, Wily Weasel!

Once Binkle and Flip Bunny were walking home together through the snow, when they met Hasty Hare. He was lying in the snow, kicking up his legs and laughing till the tears ran down his whiskers.

'What's the joke?' asked Binkle Bunny.

Hasty sat up, still laughing. 'Well, you know old Wily Weasel?' he said. 'He's always chasing after us. I've just played a trick on him!'

'What did you do?' asked Flip.

'I got up on the roof of his house, which was piled high with snow,' said Hasty. 'And I waited there with a broom till he came out – then – *Whoooooooosh!* I swept all the snow on top of him, and you should have heard him yell! I laughed so much that I fell off the roof on top of him.'

'He'll be after you then,' said Binkle, looking round in alarm, because he didn't like Wily Weasel at all.

'Oh, he thinks it was one of *you*,' said Hasty, with another giggle. 'I heard him yell out, "I can see you, Binkle – or is it Flip? One of you! I'll be after you both." Ho, ho, ho, really it *was* a joke!'

Hasty Hare loped off, still laughing. But Binkle and Flip weren't laughing at all. They looked at one another.

'It *was* a funny joke,' said Binkle, fearfully. 'But I do hope Wily didn't *really* think it was us!'

'Look – is that Wily coming – over there?' cried Flip, in great alarm. 'Run, Binkle, run!'

They ran – but Wily could run faster. He caught them up, and showed his sharp teeth. 'Oho! Now which one of you brushed that snow on to me?'

'Please – it wasn't us,' said Binkle. 'It was Hasty Hare. Really it was. He just told us.'

'We've been to tea with Robert Rabbit,' said Flip. 'You ask him. Call down his hole and see.'

Wily Weasel took them both firmly by the arm, and led them to Robert Rabbit's hole. He called down it. 'Hey, Robert Rabbit! You down there? Who came to tea with you today?'

'Binkle and Flip Bunny!' called back Robert. 'And what's it to do with you, I'd like to know?'

Wily Weasel didn't answer. He looked at Binkle and Flip out of his sharp eyes. He still held them tightly.

'Now you listen to me,' he said. 'I can't tell where Hasty Hare lives in all this snow. You know his house, and you're to take me to it – if you don't, I'll take *you* home for my dinner instead.'

'P-p-p-please let us g-gggggo!' begged Binkle and Flip.

'Oh n-n-n-n-no!' said Wily, with a horrid smile. 'Come along, lead the way.'

Binkle mournfully began to lead the way, but to his surprise Flip pulled the other way. Binkle stared at him, and Flip gave a really enormous wink. Aha! Something was up. Binkle went the way that Flip was leading, wondering where they were going.

Across the snowy field. Up the snow-drifted lane. Past the white hedges. Up the white-blanketed hill. Then Wily Weasel began to grumble.

'It's a long way. I didn't know Hasty lived so far away. Are you sure you know where he lives?'

'Just wait and see,' said Flip. 'Look — do you see that gorse bush over there, covered in snow? Well, behind it you will see a small blue door.'

'Aha!' said Wily, snapping his teeth together. 'AHA! Hasty Hare, I'm coming. You just look out!'

'Now, you listen to what I say,' said Flip. 'You don't want to give him any warning, do you, that you're coming? Else he'll be out of his back door in a twinkling. You want to go – just – like – this...'

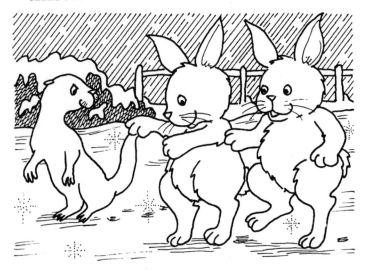

'On tippy – tippy – toe!' joined in Binkle, tip-toeing on the snow. 'Sh! Then you want to give him an awful fright.'

'Yes – you should hammer on his door, and yell, "Where are you, you scoundrel!"' said Flip.

'And then you should fling the door open, stamp in and find him,' said Binkle. 'He'll probably be in bed – so you must rip the clothes off him...'

'And give him a box on the ear – *plonk!*' said Flip. 'That will teach him never, never to sweep snow off your roof again!'

'Right,' said Wily Weasel, and he began tip-toeing through the snow to the little blue door set in the hillside behind the gorse bush. When he got there he raised his fist.

Blam, blam, blam! He hammered on that door like thunder. Then he flung it open, *crash!* – and stamped into the little house. He came to a bedroom – and sure enough there was someone cuddled down in the bed.

Wily ripped off the bed-clothes, and hit out with his paw – *biff!* 'That will teach you to bury me in snow!' he shouted.

But oh my, oh my, what was this? It *wasn't* Hasty Hare asleep in bed. It was Snarl the Wolf! Wily stared down in the greatest alarm.

'UrrrrrrrRRRRRRRRR!' growled Snarl, and leapt out of bed.

Outside the wolf's house Binkle and Flip hid under the gorse bush and listened in fearful delight. *Biff! Thud! Smackity-smackity!* UrrrrRRRRRRR. *Blam, slamity-slam, BIFF.* Whatever could be going on there? How they longed to peep in and see – but they didn't dare even to show a whisker round the door!

And then Wily Weasel came flying out of the door, yelling loudly. He landed right in the middle of the gorse bush and yelled again. Then he made off home, limping and crying.

'UrrrrrRRRRRRRRRR,' said Snarl the Wolf, and slammed his door. *Blam!*

Binkle and Flip began to laugh. They rolled about under the bush till Binkle got badly pricked, and then they went home. Oh, what a joke to tell Hasty Hare!

And now Wily Weasel is looking for Binkle and Flip as well as Hasty Hare. But do you suppose he will find them? I don't think so!

The Meddlesome Butterfly

There was once a white butterfly who was very meddlesome. If there was something it could poke its feelers into, it would! The brownies and the pixies used to be very annoyed with it when it flew in at their windows to see what cakes they were baking that day or who they were having to tea!

One day the brownie Lightfoot thought he would decorate his house from top to bottom. As he lived in a tiny house under the hawthorn hedge and had only two rooms, this was not a very big job.

I'll shut my doors and windows, and do the work without telling *anyone*, he thought. Then I'll give a party, and how surprised my friends will be to see my house all bright and new inside!

So he shut the doors and windows and set to work. He was fond of bright colours, so he decided to paint his bedroom green and his kitchen orange. My word, what a busy time he had!

He didn't go out to shop. He didn't go out to buy a newspaper or hear the news. He sent his friends the earwigs, the spiders and the butterflies to get him all he wanted. But he wouldn't let the meddlesome white butterfly do anything, because Lightfoot knew perfectly well that once that butterfly got his long feelers inside the door he would smell out his secret, and would tell everyone how Lightfoot was painting his house – and then it wouldn't be a surprise any more.

This made the white butterfly very angry. And one night when Lightfoot was in bed the butterfly flew softly down to the tiny house on his powdery wings and pushed at the door. For once Lightfoot had forgotten to lock it, and it opened. The butterfly went inside.

He went round and round the kitchen looking for matches to light a candle. His wings brushed against the walls as he felt for a shelf where the brownie might keep his matches.

He knocked over a bottle of milk. He blundered into a basket of eggs and upset those. Crash! That frightened him, for he heard Lightfoot jumping out of bed. He scurried to the door, knocking over a pot of paint on the way. Meddlesome little butterfly!

Lightfoot was so angry in the morning when he found his eggs broken, his milk upset and his paint overturned.

He asked everyone who it was that had done so much damage, but no one had any idea at all.

The meddlesome butterfly felt quite sure that nobody would guess it had been him in the little house. So he spread his wings boldly and flew down to the crowd of people round Lightfoot's house.

And as soon as he sat beside them everyone knew that it had been the meddlesome butterfly who had been in Lightfoot's house. How did they know?

Yes – the tips of his wings had brushed the wet paint on the wall and had coloured them orange! 'It's you who was here last night!' cried Lightfoot in a rage, and caught him and used him to fly on for the rest of the summer.

The Little Toy Farm

There was once a little boy who had fifty pence given to him every Saturday by his uncle for running errands in the week. Timmy had no father and no mother, and his uncle kept a toy shop in the village. His aunt was a cross old woman who never made a cake and thought jam was horrid.

So Timmy didn't have a very good time – but he was quite happy all the same, for he loved playing with the toys in the toy shop and was very sorry when any of them were sold.

Then one day a dreadful thing happened. Timmy was playing with his favourite toy, a lovely toy farm with all kinds of animals in it – when suddenly a beautiful fairy doll, sitting all by

43

herself on a high shelf, fell over on to the floor.

SMASH! Her lovely face broke into a hundred pieces, and her arms and legs broke in half. Timmy stared at her in dismay, and then the door was flung open and his uncle and aunt came running into the shop to see what was the matter.

'You naughty little boy!' cried his aunt, when she saw the broken doll. 'That doll was worth five pounds! And you've broken it! I've always said your uncle was silly to let you play with the toys.'

'I didn't break it, Aunt,' said Timmy, frightened. 'It just fell down. Really it did.'

'Don't tell naughty stories,' said his uncle, angrily. 'Dolls don't fall down by themselves. Go out of the shop at once, Timothy. You are never to play with any of the toys again.'

'But, Uncle, can't I play with the lovely toy farm?' asked Timmy. 'Look, I've been so careful with it, I haven't broken even a leg off a horse.'

'You'll just come straight out of here and go to bed,' said his aunt, 'and you'll not play with any more toys at all, Timothy, so don't say another word. If you want any toys you must buy them with your pocket-money, like other children. You've been spoilt, but you won't be any more!'

So poor Timmy had to go straight upstairs to bed for the rest of the day, though he hadn't broken the doll at all. It had been the doll's own fault, really, because she had tried to see what Timmy was doing with the toy farm, and she had leaned too far over and had fallen down to the floor. But nobody knew that.

What worried Timmy was that he wouldn't be able to play with the toy farm any more. He loved that farm. It had a nice little farmhouse that you could build up yourself. You had to put the little glass windows in and everything, and set the two chimneys on the roof. Then there were fences that you could build round the farm, and make any shape you liked. There were two ploughs, six horses, twelve sheep, lots of ducks, hens, turkeys, and five little pigs.

'Then there were the two goats,' said Timmy to himself, as he lay in bed thinking of it. 'And the little dog I called Rover, and the two cats. And there was the donkey and two calves. And I had just built up such a nice stable for the horses and a lovely sty for the pigs. Oh, I do think Uncle might have let me go on playing with it. I always put it away nicely and never broke anything at all.'

The Little Toy Farm

Timmy wasn't very happy after that day, because he had no toys to play with at all. He only had two books and he had read those so often that he knew them by heart. Then he suddenly had a good idea.

'Uncle gives me fifty pence a week. Why shouldn't I buy a toy farm for myself, bit by bit?' he thought. 'Aunt makes me put my money into my money-box each week – but surely she would let me spend it on Uncle's toys.'

So he went to ask his aunt if he might. But she was cross that day, and said no, certainly not, he was getting too big to play with toys.

'Please, Aunt,' said Timmy. 'Please do let me. I'm not eight years old yet, and all the other boys in my class at school have toys to play with.'

'Well, you can have half your money to spend each week, if you like,' said his aunt at last. 'You must put twenty-five pence in your money-box, and the other twenty-five pence you can spend in the shop. It's going back into your uncle's pocket, so I don't expect *he* will mind!'

Timmy was very glad. That Saturday he put twenty-five pence into his money-box and then went into the shop to see what he could buy. Should he buy a horse, or three hens or two sheep? Or should he buy nothing at all but save his money until he could buy the cardboard, wood, bits of glass and chimneys to build the farmhouse?

'I must have something to begin with,' said Timmy, and he bought two sheep, which he stood on his mantelpiece and looked at every day. They were the first beginnings of his very own farm.

Then for eight weeks he saved his money till he could buy the stuff to build the farmhouse. After that he bought animals and farm birds, and soon, bit by bit, his farm grew. He put it on his bedroom table, and played with it every day.

He bought fences and ploughs, little trees in wooden tubs, a pigsty and a stable for the horses. He filled a tin-lid with water and made a pond for the ducks to swim in. It really was a lovely farm.

And then, just as Timmy had got it all complete, his uncle said he was going to be sent away to school!

'But Uncle! Why can't I go to school in the village, where I've always been?' asked Timmy. 'Oh, please don't send me away.'

'You are old enough to go to a boarding-school now,' said his uncle. 'But you may come home each Saturday, and spend the weekend here, if you like.'

So Timmy had to make up his mind to go away. He was sorry to leave his toy farm. He was dreadfully afraid that his aunt would sweep it all away, or give it to someone she knew in the village, as soon as he was gone.

'It worries me very much,' said Timmy to himself. 'I've spent all my money on it for I don't know how many weeks – and now, just as it's finished and looking perfectly beautiful, I've got to go away and leave it. It's really too bad.'

He wandered out into the garden, and went down to the wall at the bottom. It was a very beautiful old wall, and glowed red in the sunshine. It was planted with moss here and there, and had all kinds of delicate little plants in the crevices and corners.

Timmy leaned on the wall - and then gave a jump - for someone with a very high, shrill voice shouted right into his ear.

'Hi! Don't lean just there, if you don't mind. I've planted a nice bit of moss in that corner this morning.'

Timmy stood up and looked to see who spoke – and dear me, he *was* surprised! For standing on the top of the wall with a very tiny wheelbarrow was the smallest man you could imagine. He really wasn't more than ten centimetres high, and he wore an old green suit with a leather apron at the front. He had a spade in his hand, and he was looking very serious indeed.

'Who are you?' said Timmy, in astonishment. 'I've never in my life seen anyone so tiny. Are you real?'

'Real? Of course I'm real!' said the tiny man with a laugh. 'I'm the wall-gardener. Who did you think kept the wall in such good order? Who did you think planted the moss and all the tiny plants here? Who do you suppose kept everything tidy and nice on the old wall? Why, *I* do, of course!'

Well, Timmy was so astonished that he couldn't think of anything to say, and he just stood and stared at the tiny fellow on the wall. The little man was very old and rather bent. He had the jolliest smile and lovely twinkly eyes. Timmy liked him very much.

That was the beginning of the friendship between Timmy and Mr Jollyface, the wall-gardener. Each day they talked to one another, and soon knew all about each other.

Then one day Mr Jollyface met Timothy with a sad look in his twinkly eyes.

'What's the matter?' asked Timmy.

'Oh, I've just had a letter from Fairyland to say that I'm too old now to go on with my job,' said Mr Jollyface, sadly. 'They're going to send someone else to do it, and I've got to retire and go back to Fairyland.'

'Well, of course I shall miss you terribly,' said Timmy. 'But won't you like going to live in Fairyland with all your friends?'

'Not a bit,' said Mr Jollyface. 'You see I've been doing this job for a hundred years now, and I was on another wall for two hundred years before that, till it fell down. So I've quite forgotten what Fairyland is like, and as for my friends, why they'll all have forgotten me by this time. The friends I like are the robins and the thrushes, the squirrels and the hedgehogs in your garden, Timmy – and you.'

Timmy was very sorry for Mr Jollyface, and he told him so.

'I've got troubles too,' said Timmy. 'You know, I've a beautiful toy farm that I bought all by myself and built up bit by bit. And now I've got to go away to school and leave it – and I'm so afraid my aunt will break it all up when I'm gone, or give it away. I do wish I could find someone who would look after it for me.'

The little man stared at Timmy, and Timmy stared at the little man – and the wonderful idea came to them both at the same time.

'Ooh!' said Timmy. 'I wonder if *you'd* like to look after it for me, Mr Jollyface. You could live in the farmhouse, and you'd have all the horses, pigs and hens for company.'

'Wouldn't that be *wonderful!*' said Mr Jollyface. 'I don't want to go back to Fairyland a bit, but I've nowhere else to go – and if I could only live in your little farmhouse, that would be exactly right for me. But, you know, you'd have to bring it all out of doors, for I couldn't live indoors.'

'That's easy,' said Timmy. 'I could pack everything into a big box, and carry it anywhere you please. Where would be a good place?'

'Well, I know of a nice little dell in Wishing Wood nearby,' said Mr Jollyface, excitedly. 'You could put the toy farm there, and I could look after it splendidly, because I know nobody would ever see it in this place I am thinking of.'

'When do you have to stop your job and give it to the next wall-gardener?' asked Timmy.

'On Thursday,' said Mr Jollyface.

'Well, I don't have to go away to school till Saturday,' said Timmy. 'So on Thursday I'll pack up all the things, and take them to the wood. You can show me the way. Then we'll have plenty of time to build the farm for you.'

The two were so excited when Thursday came. Another tiny wall-gardener had come to take Mr Jollyface's place, and was at work on the wall. Mr Jollyface had packed up all his belongings, which weren't many, and had piled them in his wheelbarrow. He was waiting for Timmy at the bottom of the wall.

The little boy had carefully taken his toy farm to bits and put it into a big cardboard box. His aunt had seen him and had wanted to know what he was doing.

'Oh, I'm going to give it to someone,' said Timmy.

'And a good thing too,' said his aunt. 'I should have taken it all down and thrown it away myself, if you hadn't cleared it up. It's quite time you stopped playing with toy farms and thought more about your lessons.'

Timmy said nothing more. He ran off down the garden with the box, and then he and the tiny man went towards Wishing Wood, with Mr Jollyface leading the way. They went down a narrow, twisting path, and at last came to a nice little dell.

'Here it is,' he said. 'Now what about putting the toy farm here, Timmy?'

'It's a lovely place for it,' said the little boy. 'I'll build the farmhouse for you straight away. Then you can live in it tonight.'

So he built it up. Mr Jollyface watched, and thought Timmy was very clever. He loved the two chimneys, and when he found that he could really look through the windows he was delighted.

'But where shall I sleep?' he asked, peeping out of the front door of the house. 'I couldn't bring my little bed with me because I had to let the other gardener have it.'

'I'll buy you a doll's bed out of my uncle's shop,' said Timmy. 'He's got a nice one there for ten pence.'

On Friday the two friends set up the fences round the farm, and built the pig-sty and the stables. Then they put out all the animals. The farm was finished! The tiny trees stood about in their tubs, and the ducks floated on their tin-lid pond. Mr Jollyface thought everything was lovely.

'Next time you come you'll get a surprise,' he said to Timmy. 'I'm going to send to Fairyland for a bit of magic!'

Then Timmy had to say goodbye to Mr Jollyface, for his aunt had told him to be in early on Friday so that she might help him to pack his things for the next day. On Saturday Timmy went to the station and was put on to the train for his new school – and all the way there he was wondering how little Mr Jollyface was getting on at the toy farm.

The first week at school seemed a very long time. Poor Timmy got into trouble with his sums. He just *couldn't* get them right, no matter how hard he tried. It was such a nuisance, and the master got very angry with him.

Saturday came at last and Timmy went to the station to catch the train home for the weekend. He wondered and wondered how Mr Jollyface had got on – and tried to think what the surprise was that the little man would have to show him.

As soon as he had seen his aunt and uncle, Timmy ran off to Wishing Wood and went to the little dell – and there he saw his toy farm – but it wasn't a toy one any longer! It was certainly just as small – but whatever *do* you think. The little man had sent for some magic and had used it to make all the animals and birds come to life!

'My goodness,' said Timmy, in surprise and delight. 'Look at my horses eating the grass! And what a noise those pigs are making! And look at the hens scratching for grain, and the ducks really swimming! Mr Jollyface, where are you?'

The tiny man came running out of the farmhouse in delight.

'What do you think of it all?' he asked. 'Do you like it, Timmy? Doesn't it all look lovely now the animals are alive? And do you see I've made those wooden trees really grow? And I've planted a lot of my seeds all about so that very soon I shall have a lovely garden round the farmhouse. Oh, Timmy, I'm so happy, really I am.'

'It *does* look nice,' said Timmy, looking at the toy farm in wonder. 'Oh, I *am* glad I brought it here for you to live in, Mr Jollyface, for I'm sure you will take great care of it.'

'Yes, I will,' said Mr Jollyface. 'I shall paint the farmhouse when it needs it, and plough up part of the ground to grow vegetables, and keep the stables nice and clean. I am very proud of living on such a beautiful farm.'

All that day and the next Timmy spent with Mr Jollyface on the farm. It was most exciting to arrange the fences again and to put the pond in a better place, because there were really live animals to move about too. Timmy *did* enjoy himself.

He spent his twenty-five pence on a table and two little wooden chairs that week, and gave them to Mr Jollyface to put in the farmhouse. The little man was very grateful, and fished in one of his pockets for something to give to Timmy in return. He brought out a pencil, very small but with a very sharp point.

'Use this at school,' said the little man. 'It will be useful to you.'

Timmy had to go back on Monday, and he took the pencil with him – and do you know, all his sums came right that week, and he didn't make a single mistake in his dictation either! I think it must have been the pencil that Mr Jollyface gave him, don't you?

The Little Toy Farm

The little toy farm is still in Wishing Wood. Mr Jollyface still lives there and is very proud of the farmhouse, for Timmy has bought lots of furniture for it. The hens lay eggs for his breakfast, the cows give him milk, and the horses give him rides whenever he wants a canter.

'I'm the luckiest man in the world!' he is very fond of saying – and I think he's right, don't you?

The Bird Man

There was once a little boy called Ben, who loved watching the birds that flew among the trees and about the blue sky. He was a little town boy who had just come to live in the country, and often his school friends laughed at him because he didn't know as much as they did about the flowers and animals of the countryside.

When the swallows came back, Ben watched them flying high in the air, catching the insects. 'What are those birds with forked tails called?' he asked his friends. They laughed at him scornfully.

'Don't you know *that*?' they said. 'They are swallows!'

'But they are not all swallows, are

they?' said Ben, puzzled. 'Some of them seem a bit different.'

'Don't you believe it!' laughed his friends. 'All those birds with forked tails are swallows.'

All the same, Ben felt sure some of the birds were different from the others. He was standing in a field watching them one day when a bright-eyed little man came along whistling.

'What are you looking at?' he asked.

'At all those swallows!' said Ben. 'They do make such a pretty twittering sound as they fly.'

'They are not all swallows,' said the little twinkling-eyed man. 'There are three different birds up there in the sky! Can't you tell the difference?'

'Not very well,' said Ben. 'I'm really a town boy.'

'*I'll* show you the difference!' said the little man. He began to whistle in a queer twittering manner. A little bird dropped down from the sky and lay quivering in the man's outspread hand.

'Here is the real swallow, the barn-swallow who loves to build in barns and outhouses,' said the man. 'Look at his steel-blue back – his chestnut forehead and throat – and his pale underparts. See his beautiful forked tail!'

The bird flew upwards with a glad twitter, and Ben saw the flash of its pale underparts. The little man again gave a soft twittering whistle and another bird dropped down to his outspread hand. It seemed very like the barn-swallow. The man stroked the little creature lovingly. 'This is a cousin of the barn-swallow, the house-martin,' he said. 'He builds under the eaves of your houses. See his white underparts right up to his beak, and see this white patch at the bottom of his back. You can always tell him by that as he flies. His tail is not so forked as that of the real swallow.'

He sent the bird up into the air, and then uttered such a curious screech that Ben jumped. Another bird dropped to his hand, screeching just as the little man had done.

'This is a swift,' said the man. 'He is not a cousin of the swallow, yet he has the forked tail and sickle-shaped wings you see in them. He is sooty-black all over except for this white spot on his chin. Hear him screech as he goes!'

Up went the little bird, screeching madly. Ben watched him – and then he turned to the bird man. He was gone! It was most mysterious!

Anyway, I know more than country boys do now, thought Ben, pleased. I can point out the swallow, the house-martin and the swift to them, as they fly. Won't they be surprised?

The Little Green Donkey

Once upon a time there was a little green donkey who had only three legs. One leg had been broken off in a fall from the nursery table, and after that the donkey looked very strange indeed.

None of the nursery children liked the green donkey.

'Why is he *green*?' they said scornfully. 'Whoever heard of a green donkey! Don't let's play with him. He's silly!'

The donkey was hurt. He couldn't help being green and, as he had never seen a real donkey, he didn't see why he shouldn't be green, blue or yellow, or any other colour.

When he lost his leg he was sadder than ever. Nobody mended it for him, and he thought he must be a very ugly toy indeed, with only three legs. All the other toys laughed at him, and none of them wanted to play with him.

One day the three children turned out the nursery cupboard, and stood all their best toys in a row. The next best they put in a heap to be given to the gardener's little boy who was ill. When they came to the green donkey, they laughed.

'Here's the silly little green donkey again,' they said. 'What shall we do with him? Even the gardener's little boy won't want him. He's such an odd colour and he's only got three legs.'

'Throw him out of the window!' said one child. So they took the little donkey and threw him out of the nursery window, not even bothering to look where he fell.

Now it so happened that a green-grocer's cart was passing by at that moment, and the donkey fell head first into a basket of brussels sprouts. He was very frightened because he thought he would fall to the pavement, and be broken to pieces. But the greens broke his fall, and he wasn't hurt a bit.

He lay there in the basket and wondered what was going to happen to him. Nobody had ever loved him or wanted him, and he was a very miserable little creature indeed. And how dreadful it was to be thrown away!

The greengrocer took his cart back to his shop. When he got there his wife told him that an order had come for a sack of brussels sprouts, so he emptied three of his baskets into a sack and tied up the neck.

The little donkey was emptied into the sack, too. How dark it was! He couldn't think what was happening, and he did wish he could find someone to talk to. But the sprouts couldn't say a word.

Soon the sack was taken away, and the donkey felt that someone was carrying it. At last it was dumped down, and a voice said, 'There you are, cook! There's your sack of sprouts!'

The sack was undone, and the cook began to empty out the sprouts to wash them. The master of the house was giving a fine dinner to all the farm labourers on his estate, and the sprouts were to go with the roast beef and potatoes.

There was such a lot to do that the cook, the kitchenmaid and a poor old woman who had come in to help had their work cut out to get it all done in time. The old woman was set to work washing and cutting the sprouts, and it wasn't long before she came upon the little green donkey in the pile of greens.

'Goodness me, look here!' she cried, and held up the donkey for the others to see. 'Look what the grocer's put with the sprouts!'

'Throw it into the fire,' said the cook. 'It's only a broken toy.'

'Well, if you don't mind, I'll take it home to my little grandson,' said the old woman. 'It's his birthday today and the poor little chap hasn't had a single present. His father's out of work, and his mother's been ill. He'll be so pleased with the donkey.'

'Well, you take it then,' said the cook.

The old woman put it into her shopping bag, and when her work was done she took the little green donkey home with her. She called in at her grandson's cottage on the way, but he was out.

His father was there, and the old woman gave him the donkey.

'Give that to Oliver when he comes in,' she said. 'It's his birthday, isn't it?'

'Yes, poor little fellow,' said his father. 'And not a single present or cake did he get! But what a fine little donkey! I could put another leg on him, and paint him up nicely. Oliver will be so pleased!'

So the man began to mend the little green donkey. He soon fitted him with another leg, so that he could stand very well. Then he touched him up with some green paint, and set him by the fire to dry. By the time Oliver came home there was the donkey, all ready for him.

'What a beautiful donkey!' cried Oliver, picking him up. 'Oh, look, Mollie and Beth! Look at my birthday present! Did ever you see such a fine little fellow! And what a beautiful colour he is! Oh, Father, I must certainly make him a stable!'

The little donkey could hardly believe his ears. Why, he had always been laughed at and pushed to one side before – and now this little boy thought him beautiful! Goodness, how happy he was!

Oliver took the donkey to bed with him and slept with him beside his pillow. The little creature stood there all night long, ready to fight any mouse or any moth that came to disturb his master. None came, but the donkey felt very brave and happy all the same.

Then Oliver set to work to make him a stable. Oh, how grand it was! There was a manger full of real straw, and a little gate that opened into the stable. His father painted the walls a shiny brown, and put two little glass windows in. The donkey felt very proud indeed.

All the other toys wanted to be friends with him. There was a doll with one arm, a china horse without a tail, an india-rubber pig with a hole in him, and a lead soldier without a gun. The little donkey was king of the toy cupboard, and wasn't he happy! He loved Oliver, and Oliver loved him, and played with him every single day!

And one day, who should come to see Oliver's mother but the mother of the three children to whom the donkey used to belong! The children came too, and asked Oliver to show them his toys.

'This is my *best* toy!' said Oliver, and he brought out his stable. 'Look! Inside is my dear little green donkey! Don't you think he is beautiful?'

'Oh, yes!' said the three children, who thought that the donkey in the stable looked very nice. 'We wish *we* had one like that!'

And how the little green donkey laughed to himself when he heard that!

Oh, Bother My Hair!

'Oh, bother my hair!' That was what Alicia said a dozen times a day. It was thick, untidy hair, and Alicia couldn't be bothered to keep it tidy.

'You're silly,' said her mother. 'It could be such pretty, shining, curly hair if you kept it nicely, Alicia. Look at Jane's hair – so thin and straight. She would be very glad to have *your* hair!'

'She can have it!' said Alicia. 'It's awful to have hair like mine that always wants brushing and tidying and tying up.'

'*All* hair needs to be brushed and washed and kept nicely,' said her mother. 'Even Jane's, thin and straight as it is. She manages to make her hair look nicer than yours, even though she has so little of it. It's only because you are lazy and careless that you won't bother with it. It's the same with your hands and nails – always dirty and black.'

Alicia groaned. People always nagged her about being tidy and clean, and she didn't want to be. As for her hair, she simply hated it! She went to her bedroom and combed it through savagely. It was in tangles and they hurt her. She flung the comb down and it broke.

'Horrid hair! Oh, bother it! It's a perfect nuisance to me.'

The next day Alicia was to go to tea at Granny's with her mother. 'Be ready, nice and tidy, to catch the quarter-past-four bus,' said her mother.

Alicia heard her mother getting ready at four o'clock, but she was reading a book and wanted to finish the story. She finished it, looked at the clock, gave a cry and rushed to the bathroom to wash her hands.

Oh, Bother My Hair!

She looked at her hair. 'Oh, bother my hair!' she said. 'I'll never have time to do it, it's all in tangles again.' She dragged a comb through it, crammed on her hat and flew downstairs. Her mother looked at her. Alicia's hands were more or less clean, but her dress was spotted. She took Alicia's hat off and saw her untidy, tangly hair.

'Look at your hair!' she said. 'You haven't even brushed it. What will Granny say if I take you looking like that? You can't come.'

'Oh, let me go upstairs and just brush it quickly, then,' wailed Alicia, and off she flew. But the bus came at that moment – her mother got into it and off it went without Alicia!

She was angry and disappointed, because she did so love going to Granny's – and she knew Granny would have made some special chocolate biscuits for her. She ran after the bus but it wouldn't stop. Alicia cried bitterly. Horrid bus! Horrid hair! Horrid everything!

She climbed a stile nearby and went into the wood. She sat down and wiped her eyes. Then she tugged at her hair angrily.

'Bother my hair! I hate it! *Bother my hair!*'

Then, to her enormous surprise, there was a little click, a door in the oak tree opposite opened – and a small face looked out.

'Do you really hate your hair?' said the little person. 'Don't you want it?'

'I hate it!' said Alicia. 'It's nothing

but a nuisance to me. It's a great big bother!'

'Well, I'll do you a good turn then,' said the little creature, 'and do myself one at the same time. I make dolls, you know – but it's *so* difficult to get good hair for them! Now, keep still one moment, please. That's right. *Timminytotallypottyperoo!*'

The magic word made Alicia jump. She felt a cold wind round her head. Then, quite suddenly, every single one of her hairs fell off to the ground.

The little creature, who looked rather like a goblin, popped out of the tree and gathered up the heap of curly hair. 'This will do *beautifully* for my dolls!' he said. 'Thanks so much. We'll both be happier now!'

And he slammed his door and disappeared. Alicia put her hand up to her head, which felt surprisingly cold. It was bald! Not one single hair was growing there.

She didn't know what to think. She really didn't. Was she glad? Did she mind? She wouldn't have any bother with her hair now – but what did she look like?

She rushed home and looked at herself in the glass. She gave a scream. 'I
look dreadful! I'm quite, quite bald! I'm
like Grandpa – my head is round and
pink and bare. Oh, I don't like it; I want
my hair back!'

She rushed off to the wood and went
straight to the oak tree where the little
goblin lived. But although she searched
and searched she couldn't find the
door, and the goblin wouldn't open it.
No – he had got all the hair he wanted,
and he knew he shouldn't have played
such a trick on Alicia – so *he* wasn't
opening the door, you may be sure!

Alicia's mother was full of horror when she got home and saw her bald little girl. She didn't believe a word of Alicia's story, not one word. She thought it must be some dreadful disease, and she called the doctor in at once.

He was puzzled. He couldn't understand it. He didn't believe Alicia's story either, of course. But what in the world were they to do with the poor, bald child? She looked so bare and ugly, not a bit like the pretty Alicia everyone knew.

She couldn't go to school because the children wouldn't have anything to do with her. They didn't like the look of her. They wouldn't believe she was Alicia. They wouldn't play with her either, and soon the big boys called after her, unkindly: 'Baldy! Hallo, Baldy!'

'Oh, Mother, Mother, if only I could have my hair back. I'd brush it a dozen times a day, I'd wash it every week, I'd never have a single tangle in it,' wept

Alicia. But no matter how many times she went to that oak tree to beg the goblin to give her back her hair, she couldn't get him to open his door.

'I'll never get back my hair,' said poor Alicia. 'I'll be bald all my life long and have to wear a wig.'

But then something happened. Her hair began to grow again! It really did. At first it was only like a baby's down, but then it grew thicker and a bit longer. Her mother was overjoyed.

'You're going to have lots of thick, curly hair again, darling!' she said to Alicia. 'Cheer up. In a month's time you will look quite different – and in three months your hair will be as thick and curly as ever it was.'

She was right. It was. Alicia went back to school, and the children soon forgot all about the time when she was bare and bald.

But Alicia never forgot. She had been so very shocked and unhappy. Now her mother never once had to tell her to brush it and tidy it. She kept it beautifully, and it made her look prettier than ever. She knew what it was to be without hair – and she was going to take good care of her curly mop now that she had it back again.

As for that goblin, he felt very guilty about what he had done – and one day, on the doorstep, Alicia found a beautiful little doll with thick, curly hair just like hers. She knew who had sent it, of course, and she knew whose hair it was. I do, too, don't you?

Black Bibs

Once upon a time, at the beginning of the New Year, the little brown house-sparrows noticed that the starlings were growing beautiful green, violet and purple colours in their feathers. They saw that the little chaffinch had put on a much brighter pink waistcoat, and that the blackbird seemed to have dipped his beak in gold.

'Why?' they said to the starlings. 'Why?' to the chaffinch, and, 'Why?' to the blackbird.

'Because spring is coming!' they all answered. 'We shall soon be looking for our little wives – and we like to be dressed in our best then! Why don't *you* do something about it, sparrows? Cock and hen sparrows are exactly the same

Black Bibs

in the way they dress! You might at least try to dress a little differently in springtime, so that when you go wooing your mates they may think you look handsome!'

'That is a good idea,' said the cock sparrows. 'We will go to Dabble, the elf, and ask her if she'll use her dyes to colour our feathers a bit!'

So they flew off to Dabble. She was indoors and the house was shut. The sparrows hopped up the path, and were just going to ring the bell when one said, 'We haven't yet decided what colour to ask for.'

'We'll have red vests,' said a big cock sparrow.

'Silly idea!' said another. 'We don't want to look like those stuck-up robins.'

'Well, let's have yellow tails and green beaks,' said another.

'And be laughed at by everyone!' screamed a fourth sparrow. 'No, we'll have blue wings and blue chests – very smart indeed.'

'I want pink legs, I want pink legs,' chirruped another.

'Be quiet and don't be silly,' said the one next to him. 'Do you want to look as if you're walking on primrose stalks? They're pink, too.'

'Chirrup, chirrup, chirrup!' shouted all the excited sparrows at once, and each began to yell out what he wanted – red head, yellow beak, green chest, pink wings, white tail and the rest. Really, you never in your life heard such a deafening noise!

Dabble, the elf, was having a snooze on her bed. She woke up in a hurry and wondered what the dreadful noise was. She opened her window and looked out. Her garden was full of screeching sparrows, pecking at one another and stirring up the dust.

'Be quiet!' said Dabble.

'Chirrup, chirrup, chirrup,' screamed the sparrows. Then they caught sight of Dabble and shouted at her loudly: 'We want to ask you to give us something that will make us look different from the hen sparrows – blue legs, or pink wings – or something.'

'Oh, I'll give you something, all right!' said Dabble crossly. 'Come in, one by one.'

So the sparrows went in one by one at her front door – and were pushed out one by one at her back door – and when they came out they were wearing little black bibs under their chins! Yes, every one of them!

'*Babies*! Quarrelsome *babies*, that's all you are!' said Dabble, shutting the door on the last one. 'And babies wear bibs – so you can wear them too!'

And it's a funny thing, but since that day every cock sparrow has to wear a black bib under his chin in the springtime. You look and see!

The Tower in Ho-Ho Wood

There were once two little girls called Mary Ann and Mary Jane. Mary Ann's mother was dead and her father had married again. Her stepmother had a little girl of her own, just the same age as Mary Ann. She was called Mary Jane.

Now the stepmother was jealous of Mary Ann, for she was a pretty child, and merry and kindhearted. Mary Jane, her stepsister, was plain, and so sulky and bad-tempered that no one liked her. Whenever anyone came to play in the garden, it was always merry Mary Ann they asked for, and never sulky Mary Jane.

It wasn't long before Mary Ann found that she was expected to do all the housework, whilst her lazy step-sister lay in bed late and never helped at all! Mary Ann didn't mind. She went about singing gaily, and did all her work as well as she could.

But Mary Jane couldn't bear Mary Ann to be happy. She hated to hear her stepsister singing merrily. So one day, when Mary Ann had been making gooseberry jam, she crept into the kitchen and upset the pan so that all the jam was spilt on the floor and was wasted. No one saw her do this, and she ran out of the kitchen quickly.

When the stepmother came in to see what the noise was, she found poor Mary Ann crying bitterly to see her jam wasted, and such a terrible mess to clear up.

'Did you upset that, you careless girl?' cried her stepmother, and without waiting to hear the answer, she boxed her little stepdaughter's ears.

'I didn't do it!' sobbed Mary Ann. 'I'm sure it was bad-tempered Mary Jane, who did it to make me unhappy.'

'How dare you tell stories like that!' cried the stepmother, angrier than ever, and she slapped Mary Ann hard. 'You are a very naughty little girl.'

Poor Mary Ann! She spent the whole morning clearing up the mess, and then she had to go without her dinner as a punishment for spilling the jam – though of course it was really Mary Jane who had done it.

Mary Ann forgave her stepsister, and tried to be nice to her – but the more she tried the more Mary Jane hated her. Mary Ann grew prettier and sweeter, and at last the stepmother thought that she really must send her away, for her own daughter looked so cross and ugly beside Mary Ann that everyone noticed the difference.

But how could she send her away? Her father would be sure to want to know where she was, and he would go and bring her back, for he was fond of Mary Ann. At last, after a great deal of thinking, the stepmother thought of a plan. She would send Mary Ann to Ho-Ho Wood for some wild strawberries – and then perhaps she would never come back, for the Little Folk lived there, and had forbidden any mortal to set foot in their wood.

So one morning she called Mary Ann to her, and gave her a basket.

'See,' she said, 'I want some wild strawberries to make a pudding for your father. Take this basket, and go to Ho-Ho Wood where there are plenty. Do not come back until you have your basket full, or I will beat you.'

'But, stepmother, the Little Folk will not let us set foot in Ho-Ho Wood,' said Mary Ann, in terror. 'They will be very angry with me if they catch me, and perhaps they will turn me into a frog!'

'Do as I tell you,' said the stepmother,

angrily. 'You will come to no harm. Fetch the strawberries, and let me hear no more words from you.'

With that she pushed Mary Ann out of the door, and slammed it behind her. The little girl didn't know what to do. At last she decided to go towards Ho-Ho Wood, and see if there were any strawberries on the borders. So off she went, carrying her basket.

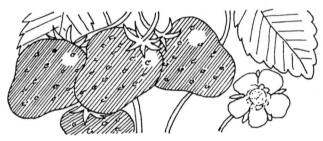

She soon came to the wood. It was thick and dark. Mary Ann hunted along the edge for strawberries, but she could see none. Just inside the wood there were plenty – she could see them through the trees. But Mary Ann didn't want to go there without permission, for she knew that the Little Folk would be angry .

She walked along the borders of the wood, wondering if perhaps she would see a gnome or a brownie whose permission she might ask. But she saw no one. Suddenly, as she turned a corner, she saw a queer little house in front of her, set on the edge of the wood. It was very small and very crooked. The little garden was set with brilliant flowers, and at the end of it stood an old well.

As Mary Ann walked up to it, she saw an old woman going down to the well with two big buckets.

I might ask her if I would be allowed in the wood, thought Mary Ann, so she went in at the gate.

'Good morning,' she said politely to the old woman.

'Dear me, how you made me jump!' said the old woman, and she dropped her buckets to the ground, and sat down in a fright on the wall nearby. 'I didn't hear you coming.'

'Oh, please forgive me,' said Mary Ann. 'Let me draw your water for you. The buckets are heavy for you to carry.'

So she let the buckets down into the

well one after the other and filled them with water. Then she carried them into the cottage for the grateful old woman.

'You are a kind little girl,' said the old woman. 'Now tell me what I can do for you.'

Mary Ann told her all about how she had been sent to get wild strawberries from Ho-Ho Wood.

'But I am afraid to go into the wood in case the Little Folk are angry with me,' she said.

'I will help you,' said the old woman. 'See, take this needle and thread, this bottle of water, and this little golden key. You will be quite safe with all these.'

'But what shall I do with them?' asked Mary Ann, in surprise.

'You will see when the time comes,' answered the old woman. 'You will be safe in Ho-Ho Wood, little girl, for you have a kind face and heart, and such folk are always welcome in the wood. It is only unkind, selfish people that come to grief.'

Mary Ann thanked the old woman very much, and then made her way to the wood. She stepped over the ditch that edged the wood, and found herself among the trees. She began to hunt for strawberries, and soon she found some. She was picking them happily, when she heard a noise behind her, and she looked round.

She saw a gnome looking at her crossly.

'What are you doing here?' he asked. 'This wood is private. I shall take you prisoner unless you can do something for me.'

'What shall I do?' asked Mary Ann, frightened.

'Can you sew six buttons on my new coat?' asked the gnome, showing her six little red buttons. 'I haven't got a needle.'

'Yes!' said Mary Ann, gladly, and she took the needle and thread that the old woman had given her, and quickly and neatly sewed the buttons on the gnome's coat, whilst he stood in front of her.

'Oh, that is beautiful!' said the gnome, pleased. 'Wait a moment, little girl. Let me touch you with my magic stick.'

He took a stick from his pocket, and touched Mary Ann with it. Immediately her ragged dress was gone, and in its place appeared a lovely one of gold and silver, set with little rubies all along the hem. Her socks changed to silken stockings, and her shoes to golden slippers with diamond buckles. How pleased and astonished she was!

'Oh, thank you!' she cried. 'What a lovely dress!'

'If you want fine strawberries go down that little path to the right,' said the gnome. 'There are some lovely ones there.'

So Mary Ann ran down the little path and soon found some very big strawberries. She had begun to pick them when a bent old wizard in a big pointed hat came striding by. He looked very hot indeed, and he was very much out of breath, for he panted like a steam-engine.

When he saw Mary Ann he stopped.

'What are you doing here?'he asked, angrily. 'Don't you know this wood is private?'

He looked so fierce that Mary Ann was frightened. Then she suddenly remembered the bottle of water that the old woman had given her. She took it out of her pocket, and held it out to the wizard.

'You look hot and thirsty,' she said. 'Drink some of this water.'

'Thank you,' said the wizard, and he took it. He drank every drop and was delighted.

'Nicest water I've ever tasted,' he said. 'You are a kind little girl. Take this in exchange for the water.'

He gave her a little bag and then marched off through the trees. Mary Ann looked at the bag. It was full of gold. She emptied the gold pieces out into her hand – and lo and behold, as soon as the bag was empty it filled itself again, and when Mary Ann looked into it she saw many more gold coins waiting for her!

'It's a magic bag!' she said in excitement. 'Oh, now I shall be rich! I shall have as much gold as I want! I can buy presents for everybody.'

She went on picking the strawberries, and wandered here and there through the wood. Suddenly she came to a little tower, which had a tiny door in one side. Mary Ann thought it was a curious place. It had no windows except one small one right at the top. The little girl put her hands to her mouth and called loudly:

'Does anyone live here?'

At that an ugly, untidy-looking boy put his head out of the window. When he saw Mary Ann standing below in her beautiful dress he was astonished. He thought he had never seen anyone so lovely in his life.

'I have been locked up here,' he said, mournfully. 'I was riding through the wood, not guessing that it belonged to the Little Folk, and the goblins caught me and imprisoned me. I have been here for a month, and I cannot get out. The door is locked fast.'

'I think I can set you free!' cried Mary Ann, joyfully, and she felt in her pocket for the little golden key that the old

The Tower in Ho-Ho Wood

woman had given her. She slipped it into the lock of the tiny door, and turned it. The door opened easily, and Mary Ann called up the spiral stairway in front of her:

'Come quickly, you are free!'

Down the stairs came the boy. He was certainly very ugly, for his nose was far too long, one eye was blue and the other brown, and his hair was thin and straggly. His clothes were dirty and ragged, and he limped badly. Mary Ann thought he was a pedlar.

'I cannot thank you enough,' he said. 'You are the kindest girl I have ever seen. Now I wonder if my horse is anywhere near here so that we may ride away from this wood in safety.'

He looked about, but all he could see was a thin donkey munching some thistles.

'This will do to carry us,' he said. 'Will you ride with me out of the wood? I know the way.'

Now Mary Ann found that she was lost, for she did not know which path to take. So, though she did not like to ride with such a dirty, ragged-looking boy, she said yes, she would go with him. She did not like to hurt his feelings by saying he was too dirty. So up she jumped behind him on the donkey and together they rode through the wood.

As soon as they had reached the borders of the wood a very strange thing happened. The donkey suddenly turned into a magnificent black horse! It cantered along, its long mane flowing in the wind, its harness glittering with silver and gold.

Mary Ann was amazed. She thought she would ask the pedlar if he had seen what had happened – and what a surprise she had! Instead of the ugly, dirty, ragged boy, she saw a handsome prince with thick curly hair, two bright blue eyes, and a merry smile. His nose was no longer too big and his teeth were white and even.

He wore a tunic and cloak of satin embroidered with gold thread, and by his side hung his sword. He looked at Mary Ann and smiled.

'I am no longer an ugly pedlar!' he said. 'I have changed back to my right form. It was kind of you to ride with me when you thought I was ugly and ragged. You have a sweet face and a kind heart. Will you marry me and be my queen?'

Mary Ann was so happy that she could hardly say yes. She fell in love at once with the handsome prince, and whispered that she would be glad to marry him. So they jogged along together very happily to Mary Ann's home.

How astonished the stepmother and Mary Jane were to see Mary Ann coming back dressed in gold and silver, sitting behind a handsome young prince! They could not believe their eyes. She jumped down from the horse and told them all that had happened.

'We will have a fine wedding!' she said. 'I have enough money in this magic purse to pay for everything. And when the wedding is over I shall go to live with my prince in his beautiful castle! Oh, look, here are your strawberries, stepmother. See what fine ones grow in Ho-Ho Wood.'

The next week the wedding was held, and folk from near and far came to it. Everyone said that the bride was the prettiest, kindest-looking girl in the kingdom, and when the prince rode off with her all the guests cheered and waved.

Only two people were angry and upset about Mary Ann's good luck, and they were her stepmother and stepsister.

'Now Mary Ann is the grandest lady in the land, and we are nobodies,' said Mary Jane, crossly.

'Listen, daughter,' said the mother. 'I have a plan. Why don't you go to pick strawberries in Ho-Ho Wood, and do all that Mary Ann did? Perhaps you also will come back with a prince and a purse of gold.'

'Very well,' said Mary Jane. She took a basket and set off. She looked for the tiny cottage Mary Ann had told her about, and soon she saw it. The old woman was going up the path to the well, and Mary Jane stepped into the garden, banging the gate so hard that the old woman jumped and dropped her two buckets.

But instead of being sorry, Mary

The Tower in Ho-Ho Wood

Jane laughed loudly, for she had no manners at all.

'You looked funny when you dropped your buckets,' said the rude little girl.

'Please fill them for me,' said the old woman. 'You gave me such a fright that I am not able to let them down into the well.'

So Mary Jane let the buckets down, and drew them up full of water. But she put them down so carelessly that they spilt over the old woman's feet and made her shoes and stockings wet. Mary Jane said nothing, but stood looking at the old woman.

'What do you want?' asked the old woman, crossly, wiping her shoes dry.

'I want the needle and thread, the bottle of water and the golden key,' said Mary Jane. 'You gave them to my sister, and she got a golden dress, a purse of gold and a handsome prince who married her. I want the same.'

The old woman laughed a low laugh. She went to her cottage and came back again with something in her hands.

'Here you are,' she said to Mary Jane, and she put into the little girl's hand a needle and thread, a bottle of water and a golden key. Then she chuckled again and went back to her cottage.

Mary Jane was delighted. Now she would soon get the same wonderful things as her stepsister! She ran down the path and into the wood. It wasn't long before she saw a gnome looking at her crossly.

'What are you doing?' he asked. 'This wood is private. I shall take you prisoner unless you can do something for me.'

'I know what you want me to do!' said Mary Jane, whipping out her needle and thread. 'Come here and I'll sew the buttons on!'

The gnome handed her six buttons in silence. She sewed them on one after another, and very badly she did it too. Three times she pricked the gnome and made him jump, and he looked as black as a thunder-cloud when she had finished.

'Now touch me with your magic stick and change my dress!' said Mary Jane. The gnome took out his stick and touched her with it – but, alas for Mary Jane! Instead of a beautiful gold and silver frock appearing, she found that her little cotton dress had changed to a thick, ugly one of grey wool, with patches here and there, and a big hole in the skirt.

How upset she was! But she had to wear it, for her cotton frock had disappeared. She went on into the wood, crying bitterly. Soon she became thirsty, and she looked about for a stream to drink from. But all she could find was a muddy ditch, and she did not want to drink from that!

'I know what I will do,' she said. 'I will drink the water out of the bottle, and fill it with ditch water. I am sure the old wizard won't know the difference!'

So she drank all the water from the bottle and then filled it up with dirty ditch water. She had hardly finished doing so when she saw the bent old wizard coming along.

'What are you doing here?' he asked, angrily. 'Don't you know that this wood is private?'

'Drink some of this water,' said Mary Jane. 'You look hot and thirsty.'

She handed the wizard the bottle and he put it to his mouth to drink – but as soon as he tasted it he knew that it was ditch water and he was angry. He emptied it on the ground.

'Give me a magic purse,' said Mary Jane.

The wizard took a bag from his pocket, and handed it to Mary Jane. Then he stalked off without a word. The little girl opened the bag eagerly – but oh, what a disappointment! Instead of being full of gold, it was full of earwigs that jumped out as soon as she opened it! She threw the bag down in horror, but after a while she picked it up again.

Perhaps it will get full of gold coins soon, she thought. Mary Ann's might have been full of earwigs at first.

So she carried it off with her. Soon she came to the little tower in the wood, and leaning out of the window at the top was a pedlar, ugly, dirty and ragged, with a long nose and one eye blue and the other brown. In a second Mary Jane fitted her key to the door and opened it. The boy came running down the stairs.

He found his donkey in the bushes and together they mounted the scraggy little beast. When they came to the edge of the wood, Mary Jane watched eagerly to see if the donkey changed to a horse – but to her great disappointment he remained a donkey. She looked up to see if the pedlar were a handsome prince – but, alas, he was still an ugly pedlar, dirty and ragged.

'I see you have a magic bag there,' he said. 'What does it contain? Golden coins?'

'Yes,' said Mary Jane untruthfully.

When the pedlar heard that, he thought that he would marry Mary Jane and then he would be rich. So he asked her to marry him and she said she would, for she felt sure that he would turn into a handsome prince sooner or later.

Soon they arrived at her home. The mother was very disappointed to find that her daughter had such an ugly dress on, and that the purse was full of earwigs. She bade Mary Jane keep the earwigs secret, or perhaps the pedlar would not marry her, and then when he turned into a prince, she would be sorry.

So Mary Jane said nothing about the earwig-purse, but made all arrangements for the wedding. It was to be the very next day, for the pedlar would not wait. So the next morning there was a wedding, and though Mary Jane told everyone that she was really marrying a prince and not a pedlar, no one believed her. They could not think that a prince would marry such a plain, bad-tempered maiden.

After the wedding the two mounted the donkey, and rode off. Mary Jane thought they were going to a palace, and she looked out for it for many hours. But at last she was tired and asked the pedlar when they would get to the palace.

'Palace! What palace?' he asked, in surprise.

'Why, *your* palace!' said Mary Jane. 'You are a prince, aren't you, and all princes live in palaces!'

'I am no prince,' said the youth. 'I am a pedlar and nothing else, as well you know. I have no money and therefore I married you, for I knew you had a bag of gold.'

'I haven't!' said Mary Jane, and she began to cry. The pedlar snatched the bag, and opened it. Out fell a crowd of earwigs, and he flung the purse on the ground in horror.

'You have deceived me!' he said, angrily. 'I would never have known you had no more gold than I. Now you will have to work hard for your living, for I am no prince, and never said I was.'

Then began a hard life for Mary Jane, for she had to work hard from morning to night and do what the pedlar told her. No longer could she be lazy, and if she sulked and frowned, she was beaten. So soon she began to learn her lesson and tried to smile and be as sweet-tempered as Mary Ann had been.

As for Mary Ann, she was living happily with her prince in his palace. All her people loved her, for her heart was as kind as her face was sweet. And one day when a pedlar and his wife came riding by her gates, she called out in surprise – for they were her step-sister and the pedlar she had married!

Mary Ann forgot how unkind Mary Jane had been to her – she forgot her selfishness and bad temper. She ran out to meet her, and hugged her lovingly. Mary Jane was humble now, and her eyes were kind. She was no longer the horrid girl that she had once been. She kissed Mary Ann, and then curtsied low to her.

'You must come and live here,' said Mary Ann. 'There is a dear little cottage nearby. You shall have it - and your husband shall be our tinker and mend all the pots and pans!'

She was as good as her word, and soon Mary Jane and her pedlar were settled happily in a dear little cottage. So everything came right, and as far as I know they are all living happily together to this day!

The Tail That Wouldn't Wag

Hidden in the thick creeper on the roof of an old thatched house was a wagtails' nest. It belonged to two wagtails, a cock and a hen. In the nest they had one baby, a fine youngster, with the most piercing voice you ever heard. In fact, it was so loud that the robins, who had a nest nearby, flew up to the wagtails in fear.

'If your nestling calls so loudly, the cats will hear and come up to find him,' they said. 'Then perhaps they will find *our* nest too, and eat up our four young ones.'

'We can't stop our chick from making such a noise,' said the wagtails. 'He is the finest, biggest, strongest wagtail in the world. Look at him!'

The robins looked. They were astonished to see such a large wagtail. He filled the nest, and his long tail stuck over the edge. He opened his orange-coloured mouth and cried so piercingly that the hen robin went off to get a caterpillar for him. He was always hungry – and even seemed to like the hairy, woolly-bear caterpillars that no other bird could eat. The robins often brought him food to make him quiet, but no matter how many grubs both the wagtails and the robins brought him, it made no difference – he squeaked just as piercingly!

When he left the nest – because he had become far too big for it – the wagtails showed him off proudly to all the other birds. They looked at the great nestling in astonishment.

'He doesn't wag his tail as you do,' said the bright-eyed blackbird. 'Why is that?'

'Oh, we are going to teach him,' said the hen wagtail hurriedly. She had not noticed this curious thing – that the fledgling's tail never wagged up and down as theirs did. So all day the two wagtails tried to show him how to wag his tail. They stood in front of him and nodded theirs a hundred times – up, down, up, down – but although the fledgling did try two or three times, his tail simply would *not* wag!

'It is so disappointing!' said the wagtails. 'He is the finest, biggest wagtail we have ever seen – and his tail won't wag!'

'Well, if his tail doesn't wag, he isn't a wagtail,' said the thrush.

'Don't be so silly!' cried the hen wagtail, in a fury. 'Didn't I bring him up myself, in our own nest? Of course he is a wagtail! I know my own child! His tail will suddenly find out how to wag – you will see it one day!'

But the young bird's tail could not wag. He gave up trying, and sat in a tree, still calling loudly for food. He was now so big that the wagtails could not reach up to his beak to feed him – so they had to stand on his shoulder and feed him like that.

The wagtails were most upset about the tail that wouldn't wag, for they were very proud of their enormous child. They called all the birds of the garden around them, and sang to them.

'Chissic, chissic! You *must* say that our youngster is a wagtail – if he isn't, then what *is* he? He must have some sort of name!'

Then a strange thing happened – the young bird made a curious sound in his throat, and then, opening his beak, he called loudly:

'Cuckoo! Cuckoo!'

'A cuckoo!' shouted everyone in great disgust. 'No wonder he couldn't wag his tail! He never will!'

And, of course, he never has!

Susan Sweet and Sally Sour

Old Man Sweet went walking down the street with his market basket on his arm. He had come out to buy his wife, Susan Sweet, a little present.

It was her birthday and, alas! Old Man Sweet only had one pound to spend! What could you get for one pound? Not very much. Old Man Sweet stood in front of the cake shop and looked at the expensive cakes there and at some big boxes of chocolates, tied up with bright ribbons.

Coming up the street was Old Man Sour. He, too, had a basket on his arm, just exactly like Old Man Sweet's. And he, too, was looking for a birthday present for his wife, Sally Sour.

What shall I buy? he thought,

jingling all the money in his pocket. Sally is so cross and grumbly, I must really buy her a mighty fine present or she'll nag at me all day!

He saw the big boxes of chocolates. He thought that the biggest one of all would be just the thing for Sally Sour. Maybe she would be so pleased with it that she would be in a good temper all day, just for once!

So he went into the shop and bought the big round box of chocolates, tied up with a bright red ribbon. The girl wrapped up the big round box in brown paper and tied it up with string. Then she put it into Old Man Sour's basket, and out he went.

Now, Old Man Sweet simply couldn't make up his mind what to spend his pound on. Not that there was much choice, because a pound really doesn't go a very long way. But at last he thought he would buy a cabbage. Yes, a cabbage would do very well, because Susan could make cabbage soup out of it, and she was very fond of that.

So he bought a cabbage, and the girl wrapped it up for him, and put it into his basket. And off he went, stepping quickly up the street.

Now at the top of the street was a seat, where people sat when waiting for the bus. Old Man Sweet sat down on it and put his basket just below the seat, to be out of people's way. He liked watching the bus come chugging up the hill, stop, let off its passengers and take in fresh ones.

Old Man Sour came up to the same seat, and he too sat down. He put his basket below the seat, just as Old Man Sweet had done, and he waited for the bus. He was going to catch it because he felt tired.

Up came the bus, clattering and rumbling. Off got the passengers, and in got the others. Old Man Sour got in last of all, carrying his basket.

But wait a minute – no, it *wasn't* his basket! He had taken Old Man Sweet's by mistake! Yes, he had – and in it was the cabbage, instead of the big box of chocolates. Well, well, what a mistake to make!

Old Man Sour didn't know he had made a mistake. Nor did Old Man Sweet, who, when the bus had gone, picked up the basket from under the seat and marched off home to his little smiling wife.

She opened the door to him and kissed him. 'You look cold, dear. I've a nice fire waiting for you, and your slippers are warming. You go and sit down and read the paper for a bit!'

'You're a dear little wife, you know, Sue,' said Old Man Sweet. 'Always cheerful and smiling, though we've been poor for years and haven't had much pleasure. I've brought you a little present, dear – but it's not much of a one!'

'Oh, you dear, generous boy!' cried Susan Sweet. 'I shall love it whatever it is. Fancy you thinking of my birthday when I'm an old woman! Now, whatever can it be?'

Old Man Sweet felt sorry it was only a cabbage. What a pity it wasn't one of those lovely boxes of chocolates! He sighed.

'Susan, dear,' he said, 'it's a poor little present – but oh, how I wish it was an expensive box of chocolates, all tied up in red ribbon!'

Susan took off the paper – and then

she gave a cry. 'Why – that's just what it *is*! A most beautiful box of chocolates! Oh, John, what a wonderful surprise!'

It was as much of a surprise to John as to Susan Sweet. He stared at the box as if he couldn't believe his eyes. How had that come there? He certainly hadn't bought it!

'Susan – I bought you a cabbage - not that box of chocolates,' he said at last. 'Is that my basket – or have I changed it by mistake for someone else's?'

They looked at the basket. No – as far as they could see it was exactly like theirs. Susan stared in delight at the box of chocolates and then she took off the lid. Oh, what a lovely sight!

'John! *I* know what's happened! Don't you remember just now saying that you wished your present was an expensive box of chocolates, all tied up in red ribbon? Well – all that has happened is – *your wish has come true!*'

There didn't seem to be any other explanation at all, so the two of them began to eat the delicious chocolates – and how they enjoyed them!

'You deserve a present like this,' said Old Man Sweet. 'You're such a nice wife to have!'

But what had happened to Old Man Sour and the basket *he* took home? Well, he travelled on the bus and unluckily he fell asleep there and went a long way past his house. So he had to catch another bus back and that made him late for his dinner.

Sally Sour met him at the door with a very cross look on her face. 'Late again! Really, I can't send you out for ten minutes without you taking two hours! What have you been doing now?'

'I fell asleep on the bus,' said Old Man Sour, feeling cross at this grumbling welcome. 'Don't nag me.'

'I shall nag you all I like!' cried Sally Sour. 'And don't you talk to me like that! I've a good mind not to give you any dinner.'

'Well! To think I went all the way down to the town and back to buy you a fine birthday present – and then I come home to be grumbled at like this!' said Old Man Sour. 'You're an unpleasant, miserable woman, Sally, and you always have been. Why can't you give a man a smile and a kind word?'

At the mention of a present, Sally Sour looked a little less cross. She grabbed the basket away from Old Man Sour.

'Don't snatch like that,' he said. 'Really, I wish I'd bought you a mouldy old cabbage instead of a fine box of chocolates!'

Sally Sour had taken off the paper – and dear me, there, sure enough, was a mouldy old cabbage! She stared in horror.

'You bought me this cabbage!' she cried. 'You mean old man!'

'I didn't. I bought you chocolates!' said Old Man Sour, astonished. 'But your bad temper made me wish I'd bought you a mouldy old cabbage –

and the wish came true. Ha, ha, that's funny. I'm very glad!'

So Susan Sweet had the chocolates and Sally Sour had the cabbage. And really, I can't help thinking that was just as it should be. They each got what they deserved – and to this day they all think that their wishes came true!

The Train That Lost Its Way

The nursery was dull and quiet. The children had gone away to the seaside, and there was nobody to play with the toys.

'There's nothing to do!' said the toy clown.

'I'm bored,' said the teddy bear. 'I don't even want to growl any more.'

'Well, that's a good thing,' said the big doll. 'I don't like your growl.'

The bear at once growled loudly. He just did it to annoy the big doll, not because he wanted to.

'Mean thing,' said the big doll, and they began to quarrel.

'You know, something must be the matter with us,' said the toy panda, looking at everyone out of his big black eyes. 'We are always quarrelling. Yesterday the clown pulled my tail.'

'And this morning the bear threw my key across the room,' said the clock-work mouse.

'And the clown smacked the big doll,' said the bear. 'Yes, something must be the matter with us.'

'I know what it is,' said the panda. 'We want a holiday! The children go away for holidays, the grown-ups go away – yes, even Topsy the dog goes away – but we don't.'

'What's a holiday?' asked the clock-work mouse.

'Isn't he a baby?' said the big doll. 'A holiday, silly, is when you leave your home and go and stay somewhere else for a change. And you come back feeling much better and you don't quarrel any more.'

'Then I should like a holiday,' said the clockwork mouse. 'Let's go and get one!'

All the toys began to feel excited. Yes, it would be great fun to go away for a holiday. But where should they go?

'To the seaside!' said the big doll.

'What's the seaside?' asked the clockwork mouse. 'Is it a kind of see-saw?'

'Of course not, baby!' said the big doll. She thought for a bit. She had never been to the seaside and she really wasn't quite sure what it *was* like.

'You'll see when you get there,' she told the clockwork mouse.

'Well, that's settled, then,' said the clown. 'We shall go away for a holiday – and we shall go to the seaside. Hurrah!'

'How do we go?' asked the bear.

'Well – the children went by train,' said the panda. 'I heard them say so.'

'Then *we'll* go by train!' said the bear. 'Where's the old wooden train? Oh, there you are. Train, will you take us to the seaside in your trucks? Do say yes. I'm sure you want a holiday too.'

'Yes, I'll take you,' said the wooden train, and it trundled up to the toys. 'I don't know the way, but we can ask. Get in.'

'What! Are we going *now*?' said the big doll. 'Gracious, I must pack.'

'What's pack?' asked the clockwork mouse. But nobody took any notice. The big doll got a bag and stuffed a lot of things into it. Then she hurried the clockwork mouse towards the wooden train.

'Get in,' she said. 'It's time we were off.'

'I'll be the guard,' said the clown, and he took a little green flag from the toy cupboard. He got into the last truck and beamed round at everyone.

'I'd better have a driver,' said the wooden train. 'I can go by myself all right, round and round the nursery, but I'd rather have a driver if we are going a long way.'

'I'll be the driver,' said the teddy bear. 'I've always wanted to be an engine-driver. Now, is everyone ready?'

The wooden train had three trucks, all of different colours. There was plenty of room in them. The panda, the pink cat, the monkey and the wooden soldier got into the first truck. The big doll, the little doll and the clockwork mouse got into the second truck.

The clown was in the last truck with the blue rabbit. They were great friends and always went everywhere together.

'Ready?' said the clown. 'Right away, then!' He waved his green flag and he blew the whistle. The wooden train, feeling very grand to have a driver and a guard, rumbled over the carpet to the door. They were off!

Out of the door went the train, and down the passage. The garden door was open and the train rattled down a little step, almost upsetting itself as it went.

'Hey! Be careful!' yelled the bear. 'I almost fell out.'

Down the garden path went the train at top speed. It was really enjoying itself. It scared two sparrows into the air and made the cat jump on top of the wall in a great hurry. Then it came out into the lane at the bottom of the garden.

'Stop a minute,' said the bear. 'Which way do we go?'

The train stopped. The monkey saw a swallow flying in the air and called to it.

'Hi, swallow! You fly over the sea

166

and back every year. Which way to the
seaside, please?'

'Take the road to the south,' twittered the swallow. 'Down the lane, that way.'

So off the train clattered again, scaring old Mrs Brown terribly when it met her in the lane.

'Now what could that have been?' she said. 'A red snake? No, there isn't such a thing.'

Down the lane and round the corner and into the wood. 'Keep to the path, wooden train, or we'll all be jerked out!' cried the bear. 'It's so bumpy off the path.'

The train was now on a little rabbit-path – and dear me, the path led right to a rabbit-hole! The train didn't stop when it came to the hole – it rushed straight down it!

It was dreadfully dark in the burrow. All the toys yelled out in fright. 'Where are we going? Stop, train, stop!'

'It's all right!' shouted the train. 'It's only a tunnel. Didn't you know that trains ran through tunnels? We'll soon be out in the open again. Don't worry, now, we shall soon be out in the sunshine.'

But, of course, they went deeper and deeper down, and very soon the wooden train and all its passengers were quite lost.

The teddy bear made the train stop. 'We'll be in the middle of the earth if you go on like this,' he said. 'Now, look – here comes a rabbit. We'll ask him the way.'

The rabbit was very surprised to see the train down the burrow. 'Trains aren't allowed down here,' he said. 'You'd better go back.'

'Can't,' said the train. 'I can only go forward.'

'Well, if you go on you'll come to Toadstool Town,' said the rabbit. 'The pixies live there. They will tell you the way to go if you ask them.'

So on went the train again at top speed, along the dark tunnel. Then, quite suddenly, out it came into the sunshine.

'Dear me, how bright it seems!' said the big doll, blinking. 'Teddy bear, I don't think much of you as a driver. I'm sure this isn't the way to the seaside.'

All round them were big toadstools.
The little doll was excited to see them,
because she was small enough to knock
at the door of one!

'It's a little house!' she said. 'Look,
it's got a door in the stalk – and a tiny
stairway goes up to the top.'

The pixies came crowding round the train. It was panting and puffing with its quick run.

'Stop here and have a meal with us,' said the pixies to the toys. 'Then we will tell you the way to the seaside.'

So all the toys sat down and had a lovely meal with the pixies. The little doll tried to get one of them to give her a pair of wings, but she wouldn't.

'You might buy a pair in the next town, where there is a market,' she said. 'Mine wouldn't fit you.'

'Time to get on,' said the wooden train, feeling tired of staying still. 'All aboard, please!'

'Listen – I'm the guard, not you,' said the clown. '*I* have to say that. Now – is everyone ready? Off we go again!'

And off they went, this time to the next town, where there was a market. Everyone wanted to buy something.

It was a brownie market. The little doll didn't much like the look of some of the long-bearded brownies. But she got out of the train with the rest.

As soon as the brownies saw the little doll they loved her. 'Catch her!' they cried. 'We'll keep her here with us. Stay here, little doll, and you shall have a new dress and a pair of wings and a lovely ring.'

'No, no!' cried the little doll, and she ran away. But the brownies ran after her, and goodness knows what would have happened if the wooden train hadn't suddenly rushed at the brownies, and knocked them over like skittles.

The toys piled themselves quickly into the trucks. The clown waved his flag and blew his whistle, and the train rattled off at top speed. The brownies couldn't possibly catch it.

'I didn't buy any wings, after all,' wept the little doll. 'Oh dear, I was so frightened.'

'Sit on my knee,' said the big doll. 'You will be all right when we get to the seaside.'

But dear me, the train had been in such a hurry to leave the brownies behind that it had taken the wrong road, and had now lost itself again.

It came to an enormous hill. 'You can't climb this, train!' said the teddy bear. But there was no other way to go.

So up the hill puffed the little wooden train, dragging the trucks behind it. And at last it came to the top.

There was a pretty little cottage there, and the toys wanted to stop and ask the way of the kind-looking old woman at the gate.

But as soon as the train ran over the top of the hill it began to rush downwards and couldn't stop!

'Stop, stop!' yelled the bear, as they went faster and faster and faster. But it was quite impossible to stop, and the toys all clutched the sides of their trucks and wondered what was going to happen.

'There's a big pond at the bottom of the hill,' groaned the bear. 'We shall run straight into it, and sink to the bottom!'

'I want to get out!' wailed the clock-work mouse. 'I don't like going so fast.'

But SPLASH! Into the water they

went. Everybody expected to sink to the bottom, and get soaking wet.

But the engine and trucks were made of wood, so of course they all floated beautifully. The trucks sailed along like little boats!

'Good gracious, whatever next!' said the big doll. 'Rushing down tunnels, escaping from brownies, panting up hills, tearing down them, sailing on ponds! What behaviour!'

There were some big white ducks on the pond. They didn't like the train splashing into their pond at all. They sailed up, quacking angrily.

'Peck that monkey! Peck that bear! Peck that mouse!' they cried. But the panda pulled up a reed growing in the pond and began to lash out at the big ducks.

'Go away or I'll whip you!' he said. 'Grrrrrrrrrr!'

The ducks sailed a little way away. 'Let's make big waves and upset them,' said one duck. So they made big waves — but the waves took the engine and the trucks to the shore, and soon the train was on dry land once again.

'Thank goodness,' said the big doll. 'Now, train, do try to go slowly and don't get us into trouble any more.'

The train was wet and cold and rather tired. So it did go slowly. It went on and on and at last ran over something yellow and soft.

'What is this stuff? It looks like sand,' said the bear. 'Better get out of it, train, or your wheels will sink into it and you won't be able to move.'

That was just what did happen. The wheels sank into the sand, and the train felt too tired to drag them out. So there it stood, quite still.

The toys got out. 'I wonder where we
are?' said the clown to the rabbit.
'What's that noise?'

Now, although the toys didn't know
it, they had come to the seaside. They
were on the sandy beach, and far down
it was the sea. The tide was out, but it
was just coming in.

The toys could hear the sound of the
waves breaking, but they didn't know
what it was. They all wandered about,
picking up shells and bits of seaweed.

'This seems a very lonely kind of
place,' said the monkey. 'And look,
what is that far away down the sand?
Is it water?'

'Yes. Another pond, I expect,' said the pink cat. 'Well, I'm not going near it. I feel tired. I'm going to go and rest against a truck. You'd better come with me.'

So all the toys went to rest themselves against the trucks, and they fell asleep. And of course the tide came in and the waves came nearer and nearer!

One wave made such a noise that it woke the monkey. He sat up in alarm.

'Look!' he said. 'That pond has come near to us. It's got waves at the edge. It's trying to reach us!'

'It's getting nearer and nearer!' cried the teddy bear, and he jumped up. 'Oh, it's a most ENORMOUS pond. I've never seen one like it. It's trying to swallow us up!'

Splash! A big wave broke near them and ran right to the big doll's feet. It wet her toes and she screamed.

'Quick! Let's run away!' she cried. 'We'll be swallowed up by the waves if we don't.'

The bear, the monkey and the clown pulled hard at the train to make it run over the sand. At last they managed to get it to a firmer patch where the wheels did not sink in.

'Now, get in, everybody!' cried the bear. 'We're off!'

Splash! A wave ran right up to them and the train rushed away in fright. It tore up the beach and on to the roadway. It rattled along, with all the toys holding tight. Dear, dear, where would they get to next?

After a long, long time they came to a little town. The train rushed down the street, and came to an open gateway. It ran in, panting.

'I really must have a rest,' it said. 'Get out, toys, for a minute.'

They got out – and the big doll gave a loud cry. 'Why – we're in our own garden! Look – there's the rose-bed – and the garden-seat – and the children's swing! Train, you've brought us all the way back. However did you know?'

'He didn't,' said the bear. 'It was just good luck. My goodness, I'm glad to be home again. No more holidays for me!'

'I *should* have liked to see the seaside,' said the clockwork mouse, as they all went back to the nursery.

'So should I,' said the big doll. 'We'll go another day.'

'But not by train,' said the monkey. 'We'll go on the rocking-horse. He's not so likely to lose his way!'

'Well, I did my best,' said the wooden train. 'I couldn't *help* losing my way. The teddy bear should have taken me the right way!'

'Never mind – it was a most exciting journey,' said the bear. And it certainly was, wasn't it?

Lightwing the Swallow

Lightwing came out of a white egg in a nest made of mud. He was very tiny indeed, and at first he could see nothing in the dark barn where his mother and father had built their nest. But very soon his eyes made out the high rafters above him, and the beam on which his nest was put.

He looked at a hole in the barn roof through which he could see the blue sky. It was summer-time, so the sky was often blue. Lightwing crouched down in the nest with his brother and sister, and waited impatiently for his mother and father to come with titbits to eat.

He was a funny little thing, rather bare, with very few feathers at first.

But gradually they grew, and soon Lightwing and his brother and sister were fluffy nestlings, sitting with ever-open beaks waiting for flies that their parents caught on the wing outside the big barn.

Lightwing was a swallow. He had a marvellous steel-blue back, a white vest, and a streak of chestnut-red across his chest. His legs were small and his beak was wide in its gape. His wings were long and his tail was forked prettily. He longed for the day to come when he might fly off with his father and mother.

But when the day came he was rather afraid! His brother flew out of the nest and through the door as if he had been used to flying all his short life – but Lightwing and his sister sat on the edge of the nest, trembling. Their mother suddenly flew behind them and tipped them off the nest!

Lightwing fell – but as he fell he opened his wings, and lo and behold he could fly! His wings flashed through the barn door – he was up in the air and away, rejoicing to be in the clear, sunny blue sky.

He learnt to catch flies on the wing with his mouth wide open. He learnt to skim the water and pick up the flies hovering over the surface. He knew that when rain was coming the flies flew lower, and he followed them. When the weather was fine the flies flew high, and Lightwing soared below the clouds, following his food there. Then people said, 'The swallows fly high – it will be fine,' or, 'The swallows fly low – there will be rain.'

Lightwing grew strong and tireless as he flew throughout the warm summer days. But one night there was a chill in the air. Lightwing was surprised. He did not like it.

'Winter is coming!' sang the robin in his creamy voice.

'What is winter?' cried Lightwing, in his pretty twitter. 'Is it something to eat?'

One night a chill north-west wind began to blow. Lightwing felt restless. He wanted to fly somewhere, but he did not know where. He wanted to go where he could no longer feel the cold wind. He flew to the barn roof to ask his friends what to do. Hundreds of swallows settled on the old red roof. They chattered and twittered restlessly. The wind blew behind them.

And then, quite suddenly, a few swallows rose up into the air and flew southwards, with the chill wind behind them. In a few moments all the waiting hundreds had risen, too, and with one accord flew to the south.

'Goodbye!' called the robin. 'Goodbye till the spring!'

Lightwing called goodbye and flew with the others. Over land and over sea sped the swallows, as fast as express trains, to a warmer, southern land, where flies were plentiful and the sun was hot.

And there Lightwing is now – but when the spring comes again he will return, and maybe build his nest in your barn or mine!